I AM NOT A CHAIR!

Ross Burach

SCHOLASTIC INC.

FOR DREW AND TODD

ISBN 978-1-338-28584-0

12 11 10 9 8 7 6 5 4 3 2   18 19 20 21 22 23

Printed in the U.S.A.   08

First Scholastic printing, January 2018

The artist used pencil and acrylic paints colored digitally to create the illustrations for this book.

Typography by Chelsea C. Donaldson

On Giraffe's first day in the jungle . . .

he felt something wasn't right.

Can I share that chair?

EEEEENOUGH!!
I. AM. NOT. A. CHAIR!

And I'm speaking up to the NEXT ANIMAL I SEE.